THE LITTLE BOOK OF
H.P. LOVECRAFT

Published in 2022 by OH!
An Imprint of Welbeck Non-Fiction Limited,
part of Welbeck Publishing Group.
Based in London and Sydney.
www.welbeckpublishing.com

ISBN 978-1-80069-234-3

Compiled and written by: RH
Editorial: Victoria Denne
Project manager: Russell Porter
Production: Jess Brisley

A CIP catalogue record for this book is available from the British Library

Printed in China

10 9 8 7 6 5 4 3 2 1

THE LITTLE BOOK OF

H.P. LOVECRAFT

WIT AND WISDOM FROM
THE CREATOR OF CTHULHU

CONTENTS

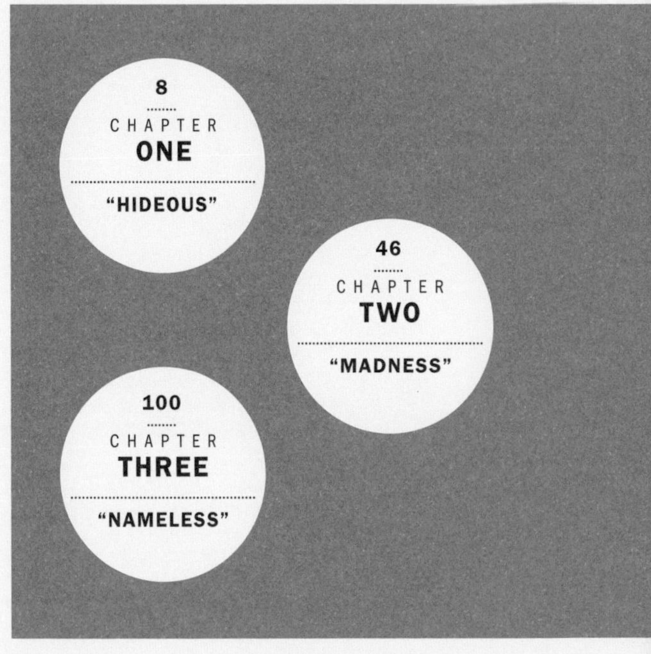

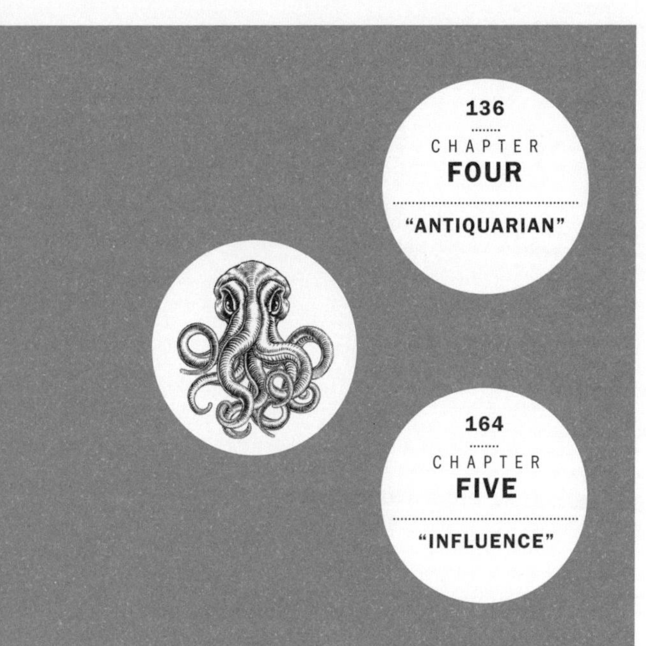

INTRODUCTION

Howard Phillips Lovecraft's writings live on long after his untimely death. His most famous creation – the Cthulhu mythos and associated world – has been added to, adapted into movies, video games, board games and influenced many other writers and disturbed millions of readers the world over.

Even Lovecraft's life was mysterious. Both of his parents were comitted to asylums during his lifetime; both died young. And the young Lovecraft had many issues with his physical and mental health. But he used all of this in his stories, many of them concerning young men from Providence – his favourite, native place – who make incredible discoveries about aliens, unspeakable horrors, nameless creatures and all sorts of nasty goings-on in the world we cannot see and do not even want to imagine. It is probably because of all his problems that Lovecraft was such a good writer. He knew about nightmares, and he realized quickly that the most powerful tool in an author's arsenal was the reader's imagination; that the most fearful being was the one that lurks deep inside all of us – the one we never want to see light of day.

Lovecraft was married, briefly, and even moved away from his beloved Providence for a while. But neither state of affairs was to last, and he returned – single – to the place he would not leave again.

But we cannot discuss Lovecraft without mentioning some of his truly ugly beliefs. He was racist and anti-semitic and had anti-immigrant ideas. Some of his stories even skirt around those issues, albeit subtly hidden. But this was not the core of his character, and he should not be remembered solely for his flaws. That he was a fantastic wordsmith is true, that he had a documentary narrative style which was beautifully concise and contributed to a genuine discomfort in the reader is also true.

This book celebrates the best of Lovecraft, through his writing, his quotes and his influences.

CHAPTER ONE

"HIDEOUS"

Howard Phillips Lovecraft was a largely unknown writer in his lifetime, with only a single, limited-edition book of his stories published. He wrote hundreds of thousands of words and is now world-famous for his fiction...

"That is not dead which can eternal lie;
And with strange aeons even death
may die."

"THE NAMELESS CITY", 1921
Lovecraft on death – a popular subject

Howard Phillips Lovecraft
was born in Providence,
Rhode Island, USA,
on August 20, 1890,
the only child of
Winfield Scott Lovecraft and
Sarah Susan Lovecraft.

"I am Providence."

H.P. LOVECRAFT
Letter to James Ferdinand Morton, 1926
Also the inscription on his fan-erected headstone

Lovecraft died in 1937 at the age of 46 in Providence, Rhode Island, USA, on March 15, 1937, of cancer.

His fear of doctors prevented him from seeking help.

Lovecraft married Sonia Greene in 1924, her second husband (of three).

They moved to Red Hook but within two years he was back in Providence and they separated.

"The feminine mind does not cover the same territory as the masculine, but is probably little if any inferior in total quality."

H.P. LOVECRAFT
Letter to Clark Ashton Smith, 1934

"My first positive utterance of a sceptical nature probably occurred before my fifth birthday, when I was told what I really knew before, that 'Santa Claus' is a myth. This admission caused me to ask why 'God' is not equally a myth."

H.P. LOVECRAFT
"A CONFESSION OF UNFAITH", 1922

"Is Lovecraft's life a tragedy of a stunted, broken-off personality, severely traumatized in childhood, and never to 'mature,' or is there a poignant triumph of a kind in the way in which the aggrieved, terrorized child refashions himself, through countless nocturnal-insomniac sessions of writing, into a purely cerebral being?"

JOYCE CAROL OATES
"The King of Weird", *The New York Review of Books*,
October 31, 1996

"Despite interest in H.P. Lovecraft's own relationships with women, his controlling aunts, and his limited marriage, his female characters are rarely explored critically, possibly because they are so few."

GINA WISKER,
New Critical Essays on H.P. Lovecraft,
edited by David Simmons, 2013

Lovecraft lived with his two domineering aunts in Providence.

His writing continued in earnest and he penned "The Call of Cthulhu".

He also wrote many poems, non-fiction essays and journalistic pieces.

"I cannot bear to talk much now, and am becoming as silent as the Spectator himself! My loquacity extends itself on paper."

H.P. LOVECRAFT
Letter to Rheinhart Kleiner,
23 December 1917

"My reason for writing stories is to give myself the satisfaction of visualising more clearly and detailedly and stably the vague, elusive, fragmentary impressions of wonder, beauty, and adventurous expectancy which are conveyed to me by certain sights (scenic, architectural, atmospheric, etc.), ideas, occurrences, and images encountered in art and literature."

H.P. LOVECRAFT
Notes on Writing Weird Fiction, 1933

"My coming to New York had been a mistake; for whereas I had looked for poignant wonder and inspiration in the teeming labyrinths of ancient streets that twist endlessly from forgotten courts and squares and waterfronts to courts and squares and waterfronts equally forgotten ... I had found instead only a sense of horror and oppression which threatened to master, paralyse, and annihilate me."

"HE", 1925
Lovecraft's Narrator on moving out of Providence

"Well – the train sped on, & I experienced silent convulsions of joy in returning step by step to a waking & tri-dimensional life."

H.P. LOVECRAFT
On moving back to Providence.
Letter to Frank Belknap Long, 1926

"I very much doubt that the illness of Lovecraft's mother had any direct relation to Lovecraft becoming a writer. He was an incredibly precocious boy and was already writing prose and verse at the age of six."

S.T. JOSHI
On H.P. Lovecraft's early years and writing, 2017

Both of Lovecraft's parents were committed to the same mental institution – Butler Hospital in Providence – separately: his father in 1893, his mother in 1919.

Relatively little of Lovecraft's work was published during his lifetime; even less was successful: "*The Case of Charles Dexter*" *Ward* was never even typed up.

"The appeal of the spectrally macabre is generally narrow because it demands from the reader a certain degree of imagination and a capacity for detachment from every-day life."

H.P. LOVECRAFT
On horror fiction
"*Supernatural Horror in Literature*", 1927

Yog-Sothoth by Dominique Signoret. Wikimedia Commons.

"I wish there could be a single writer with the sheer genius of Poe, the imaginative scope of Blackwood, and the magical prose of Dunsany!"

H.P. LOVECRAFT
On his ideal literature
Letter to August Derleth, 1932

"Poe was my God of fiction."

H.P. LOVECRAFT
On Edgar Allan Poe
Letter to Rheinhart Kleiner

"It is a mistake to fancy that horror is associated inextricably with darkness, silence, and solitude."

"COOL AIR", 1928

"Truly, Dunsany has influenced me more than anyone else except Poe – his rich language, his cosmic point of view, his remote dream-world, & his exquisite sense of the fantastic, all appeal to me more than anything else in modern literature."

H.P. LOVECRAFT
On literary influnce and style
Letter to Clark Ashton Smith, 1923

"It is fair to say that Lovecraft's work is deeply pessimistic and cynical, challenging the values of the Enlightenment, Romanticism and Christianity."

DAVID STUART DAVIES

"Smith is an American Baudelaire – master of ghoulish worlds no other foot ever trod."

H.P. LOVECRAFT
On Clark Ashton Smith
Letter to Rheinhart Kleiner, 1921

Lovecraft's first story –
written around the age of
seven – was called
'The Noble Eavesdropper'.
No copies exist.

"The sciences, each straining in its own direction, have hitherto harmed us little; but some day the piecing together of dissociated knowledge will open up such terrifying vistas of reality, and of our frightful position therein, that we shall either go mad from the revelation or flee from the deadly light into the peace and safety of a new dark age."

"THE CALL OF CTHULHU", 1926

Lovecraft's fiction is so well realized it sounds like credible non-fiction

Lovecraft's literature and style was influenced by Lord Dunsany, Arthur Machen, Clark Ashton Smith and Edgar Allan Poe.

"For the dead in their shrouds
Hail the sun's turning flight,
And chant wild in the woods as they dance
round a Yule-altar fungous and white."

"YULE HORROR" WEIRD TALES, 1926

H.P. Lovecraft reputedly wrote more than 80,000 letters. Fewer than 20,000 are believed to have survived.

Many are available digitally in the Brown University Library.

"Yet if Lovecraft is an icon he is an increasingly problematic one. This scion of a once wealthy Providence, Rhode Island family fallen on hard times was a bug-eyed racist who appeared to live in genuine fear of the Anglo-Saxon bloodline becoming tainted with corrupting influences."

ED POWER
The Irish Times, 2020

H.P. Lovecraft held some deeply racist and disturbing views.

Some of his essays expounded very unpleasant ideas, even adjusting for the standards of the day.

"There can be no doubt that Lovecraft's work challenges the dull imagination, expands expectations and attempts to create landscapes and creatures of unique and disturbing qualities."

DAVID STUART DAVIES

"My name is Jervas Dudley, and from earliest childhood I have been a dreamer and a visionary."

"THE TOMB", 1917

H.P. Lovecraft's characters often shared his personal traits – Lovecraft himself was troubled by nightmares

"One can never produce anything as terrible and impressive as one can awesomely hint about."

H.P. LOVECRAFT
Stating that it was clear he did not favour obvious blood and gore in horror...

"Lovecraft's works paint a collectively bleak picture – to say the least – one in which the entire human project is little more than a temporary, fragile moment in a universe ready to pull it asunder."

MARK PRITCHETT
Wellington Today, 2020

CHAPTER TWO

"MADNESS"

Lovecraft's fiction was published in magazines during his lifetime but subsequent generations have come to appreciate him as a master of truly disturbing fiction, categorized as horror but crossing other, fantastic boundaries.

"For those who relish speculation regarding the future, the tale of supernatural horror provides an interesting field."

H.P. LOVECRAFT

On his writing – he was constantly critical of his own work

"The oldest and strongest emotion of mankind is fear, and the oldest and strongest kind of fear is fear of the unknown."

H.P. LOVECRAFT

On fear – a sentiment he wrote about repeatedly, and on which he was an expert
"Supernatural Horror in Literature", 1927

Lovecraft was a hugely prolific writer and also wrote for others.

He even penned a story for Harry Houdini: "*Imprisoned with the Pharaohs*".

"Cosmic terror appears as an ingredient of the earliest folklore of all races, and is crystallised in the most archaic ballads, chronicles, and sacred writings."

H.P. LOVECRAFT
On the ancient sources of scaring people
"*Supernatural Horror in Literature*", 1927

"We were to face a hideously amplified world of lurking horrors which nothing can erase from our emotions, and which we would refrain from sharing with mankind in general if we could."

DR WILLIAM DYER,
"AT THE MOUNTAINS OF MADNESS", 1931

Common to Lovecraft's heroes, Dr William Dyer is a man of inner strength and (soon) a disturbing secret

An Old One. Tom Ardans' artwork based on H. P. Lovecraft's short novel At the Mountains of Madness. Wikimedia Commons.

"I have seen beyond the bounds of infinity and drawn down daemons from the stars ... I have harnessed the shadows that stride from world to world to sow death and madness..."

TILLINGHAST,
"FROM BEYOND", 1920

H.P. Lovecraft's characters had a tendency to learn too much...

"Wonder had gone away, and he had forgotten that all life is only a set of pictures in the brain, among which there is no difference betwixt those born of real things and those born of inward dreamings, and no cause to value the one above the other."

"THE SILVER KEY", 1926

Lovecraft writes on man's own internal sources of fear

"Now all my tales are based on the fundamental premise that common human laws and interests and emotions have no validity or significance in the vast cosmos-at-large."

H.P. LOVECRAFT
On the insignificance of man in a wider, universal context – another long-running theme in his work
Letter to Farnsworth Wright, 1927

"Man rules now where They ruled once; They shall soon rule where man rules now. After summer is winter, and after winter summer. They wait patient and potent, for here shall They reign again."

THE NECRONOMICON,
"THE DUNWICH HORROR", 1927

Writing on the longevity of man – and what lies in wait

"There was a kind of intoxication in being lord of a visible world (albeit a miniature one) and determining the flow of its events."

H.P. LOVECRAFT
On the pleasure of writing
Letter to J. Vernon Shea, 1933

"But the horror, set and stable,
Haunts my soul forevermore."

"ASTROPHOBOS"
THE UNITED AMATEUR, CIRCA 1918

"Then, as I remained, paralyzed with fear, he found his voice and in his dying breath screamed forth those words which have ever afterward haunted my days and my Nights... ! that have lived for six hundred years to maintain my revenge, FOR I AM CHARLES LE SORCIER!"

CHARLES LE SORCIER, "THE ALCHEMIST"
A revealing denouement
The United Amateur, 1916

"About this time I conceived my present fear of fire and thunderstorms. Previously indifferent to such things, I had now an unspeakable horror of them; and would retire to the innermost recesses of the house whenever the heavens threatened an electrical display."

JERVAS DUDLEY, "THE TOMB", 1917

Lovecraft suffered from frequent nightmares himself

"I alone remained, riveted to my seat by a grovelling fear which I had never felt before. And then a second horror took possession of my soul. Burnt alive to ashes, my body dispersed by the four winds."

JERVAS DUDLEY, "THE TOMB", 1917

A terrifying, fearful end

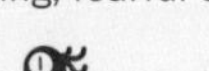

"I have said that the unbroken monotony of the rolling plain was a source of vague horror to me; but I think my horror was greater when I gained the summit of the mound and looked down the other side into an immeasurable pit or canyon, whose black recesses the moon had not yet soared high enough to illumine."

"DAGON", 1917

The unease mounts as more is revealed by moonlight

"My opened eyes sought the couch of pain in curious horror, but the blue eyes were still calmly gazing, and the countenance was still intelligently animated. He is better dead, for he was unfit to bear the active intellect of cosmic entity."

JOE SLATER,
"BEYOND THE WALL OF SLEEP", 1919

Themes of horror, life and death and a wider world are evident

"MADNESS"

Dagon by Dominique Signoret. Wikimedia Commons.

"I anything remains vague, it is only because of the dark cloud which has come over my mind – that cloud and the nebulous nature of the horrors which brought it upon me."

RANDOLPH CARTER,
"THE STATEMENT OF RANDOLPH CARTER",
1919

One of Lovecraft's first "confessional" tales

"But I do not fear him now, for I suspect that he has known horrors beyond my ken. Now I fear *for* him."

RANDOLPH CARTER,
"THE STATEMENT OF RANDOLPH CARTER",
1919

The Narrator's concerns are change

"A cry that gradually rose to a shriek fraught with all the horror of the ages–."

RANDOLPH CARTER,
"THE STATEMENT OF RANDOLPH CARTER",
1919

Verbal expressions of terror were common in Lovecraft's work...

"And then there came to me the crowning horror of all – the unbelievable, unthinkable, almost unmentionable thing."

RANDOLPH CARTER,
"THE STATEMENT OF RANDOLPH CARTER",
1919

... as was horror beyond description

"Science, already oppressive with its shocking revelations, will perhaps be the ultimate exterminator of our human species – if separate species we be – for its reserve of unguessed horrors could never be borne by mortal brains if loosed upon the world."

"FACTS CONCERNING THE LATE ARTHUR JERMYN AND HIS FAMILY"

Science was a common theme for Lovecraft – and he undertook meticulous research to lend credibility to his tales

"The room became pandemonium, and men screamed and howled in fright at the sinister being they had aroused."

"OLD BUGS", 1919

"There he would meditate upon the visions that filled his mind, and there devise the forms of beauty which later became immortal in breathing marble."

KALOS, "THE TREE", 1920

The fictional sculptor also has productive visions

"The light in the temple is a sheer delusion, and I shall die calmly, like a German, in the black and forgotten depths. This daemoniac laughter which I hear as I write comes only from my own weakening brain."

KARL HEINRICH, "THE TEMPLE", 1920

The Narrator creates his own fear

Fictional places from Lovecraft stories

Arkham

Arkham Sanitarium

Innsmouth

Kingsport

Dunwich

Miskatonic University

Martin's Beach

R'lyeh

"Contrary to what you may assume, I am not a pessimist but an indifferentist – that is, I don't make the mistake of thinking that the... cosmos... gives a damn one way or the other about the especial wants and ultimate welfare of mosquitoes, rats, lice, dogs, men, horses, pterodactyls, trees, fungi, dodos, or other forms of biological energy."

H.P. LOVECRAFT

"Life is a hideous thing, and from the background behind what we know of it peer daemoniacal hints of truth which make it sometimes a thousandfold more hideous."

"FACTS CONCERNING THE LATE ARTHUR JERMYN AND HIS FAMILY", 1920

An early hint of Lovecraft's constructed world beyond our own

"Fear had lurked on Tempest Mountain for more than a century."

"THE LURKING FEAR", 1920
Emotion is used as a character
as well as a characteristic by Lovecraft

"That I am still alive and sane, is a marvel I cannot fathom ... the shadow on that chimney was not that of George Bennett or of any other human creature, but a blasphemous abnormality from hell's nethermost craters; a nameless, shapeless abomination which no mind could fully grasp and no pen even partly describe."

"THE LURKING FEAR", 1920

Another example of Lovecraft's use of
the indescribable to engender fear in the reader

Howard Phillips Lovecraft did not receive a high school diploma, and never attended university.

"An acute terror now rose within me, for here were anomalies which nothing normal could well explain."

DELAPORE,
"THE RATS IN THE WALLS", 1922

"It had shapes, a thousand shapes of horror beyond all memory. There were eyes – and a blemish. It was the pit – the maelstrom – the ultimate abomination. Carter, it was the unnamable!"

JOEL MANTON,
"THE UNNAMABLE", 1922

"What I will do is to relate the most horrible circumstance I ever encountered, and leave it to you to judge whether or not this forms a suitable explanation of my peculiarity."

"COOL AIR"
H.P. Lovecraft sets the scene, 1926

"Then the shadows began to gather; first little furtive ones under the table, and then bolder ones in the dark panelled corners."

"THE STRANGE HIGH HOUSE IN THE MIST", 1926

"From a private hospital for the insane near Providence, Rhode Island, there recently disappeared an exceedingly singular person."

"THE CASE OF CHARLES DEXTER WARD", 1927

Rhode Island geography and institutions were common in Lovecraft's writing

"PS Shoot Dr. Allen on sight and dissolve his body in acid. Don't burn it."

"THE CASE OF CHARLES DEXTER WARD", 1927

A chilling instruction in a letter from the narrator/writer

"From even the greatest of horrors irony is seldom absent."

H.P. LOVECRAFT

"I cannot sleep at night now, and have to take opiates when it thunders."

"THE LURKING FEAR", 1922

Lovecraft was not a calm sleeper himself

"**H.P.** Lovecraft was a genius when it came to tales of the macabre."

STEPHEN KING
On Writing: A Memoir of the Craft, 2000

"Lovecraft's feebleness gave his writing its one strength: his tales can be frightening."

URSULA K. LE GUIN
The Times Literary Supplement, 1976

"Lovecraft was seeking a kind of incantatory effect in his prose, produced both by language and by incident; at times this required strong images of overt terror."

S.T. JOSHI
2017

"He's incredibly imaginative ... And all the science stuff that's in his stories is fairly accurate – he did a lot of research. For example, in *From Beyond*, he did a lot of research into the pineal gland; in *Reanimator*, he almost gives you the formula for bringing the dead back to life."

STUART GORDON
2014

“The Dark Prince of Providence.”

STEPHEN KING
On H.P. Lovecraft, in his introduction to
H.P. Lovecraft Against the World, Against Life by
Michel Houellebec, 1991

"Howard Phillips Lovecraft serves as example to all who wish to learn how to fail in life and eventually succeed in their work."

MICHEL HOUELLEBEC
From his book *H.P. Lovecraft Against the World, Against Life*, 1991

"The way he talks about his monsters – in his first description of Cthulhu he gives you a list of four things that Cthulhu isn't quite like. Which is brilliant! It's a tactic, it's not a weakness."

ALAN MOORE

From *All About Alienation: Alan Moore on Lovecraft and Providence*, by Nick Talbot

"Sadly, too many people who had never heard of Lovecraft now know him simply as a racist, rather as if Wagner were to be known purely for antisemitism."

RAMSEY CAMPBELL

"Lovecraft was a master of prose idiom: he not only had a prodigious vocabulary, but he was supremely skilled in the ability to arrange words, sentences, and whole passages such that they convey an immensely powerful impact on the reader."

S.T. JOSHI
2017

"For on the faces of this throng was writ a madness born of horror unendurable, and on their tongues were words so terrible that no hearer paused for proof."

"THE DOOM THAT CAME TO SARNATH", 1919

A scary crowd tells a wordless tale

"An American original, whose influences on subsequent writers in the field (Stephen King, for instance) is all-pervasive."

JOYCE CAROL OATES
On H.P. Lovecraft, "*DarkEcho Horror Online*", 1999

H.P. Lovecraft was a teetotaller who supported Prohibition, although he did change his mind on this in his later years.

CHAPTER THREE

"NAMELESS"

Probably Lovecraft's greatest creation was Cthulhu. A series of ancient gods that have lain in wait for mankind for centuries – and continue to do so. The Cthulhu mythos – so named after the author's death – has outlasted Lovecraft by almost a century and shows no sign of disappearing...

"The most merciful thing in the world, I think, is the inability of the human mind to correlate all its contents."

FRANCIS WAYLAND THURSTON,
"THE CALL OF CTHULHU", 1926

The Narrator sets the scene for indescribable horror

"NAMELESS"

The Madness from the Sea, Sofyan Syarief's artwork based on H. P. Lovecraft's story The Call of Cthulhu.. Wikimedia Commons

"I now felt gnawing at my vitals that dark terror which will never leave me till I, too, am at rest."

FRANCIS WAYLAND THURSTON,
"THE CALL OF CTHULHU", 1926

The creeping dread continues

"Original title *Al Azif* – azif being the word used by Arabs to designate that nocturnal sound (made by insects) suppos'd to be the howling of daemons."

"THE HISTORY OF THE NECRONOMICON", 1927

"No one, even those who have the facts concerning the recent horror, can say just what is the matter with Dunwich."

"THE DUNWICH HORROR", 1928

An entire town with a rotten core

"It was – well, it was mostly a kind of force that doesn't belong in our part of space; a kind of force that acts and grows and shapes itself by other laws than those of our sort of Nature."

"THE DUNWICH HORROR", 1928

In Dunwich there is a cosmic nature to the creatures

"Bear in mind closely that I did not see any actual visual horror at the end."

ALBERT N. WILMARTH,
"THE WHISPERER IN DARKNESS", 1930

A common theme with Lovecraft - leaving the ultimate horror to the imagination of the reader

"Mr. Wilmarth, it said, – I hope I do not startle you. I am a human being like yourself, though my body is now resting safely under proper vitalising treatment inside Round Hill, about a mile and a half east of here."

HENRY W. AKELEY,
"THE WHISPERER IN DARKNESS", 1930
A notable example of body exchange

"But to give it a name at this stage was mere folly. It looked like a radiate, but was clearly something more. It was partly vegetable, but had three-fourths of the essentials of animal structure."

WILLIAM DYER,
"AT THE MOUNTAINS OF MADNESS", 1931
Describing the early discovery

A Shoggoth. Nottsuo's artwork inspired by H.P. Lovecraft's short novel At the Mountains of Madness. Wikimedia Commons.

Cthulhu itself is a god-like being from another planet and just one of the Great Old Ones, who wait patiently to rise up and destroy the human race.

"The effect of the monstrous sight was indescribable, for some fiendish violation of known natural law seemed certain at the outset."

WILLIAM DYER,
"AT THE MOUNTAINS OF MADNESS", 1931

Another example of leaving the final horror to the reader's imagination

"Danforth refused to tell me what final horror made him scream out so insanely – a horror which, I feel sadly sure, is mainly responsible for his present breakdown."

WILLIAM DYER,
"AT THE MOUNTAINS OF MADNESS", 1931

"It was called, she said, – The Esoteric Order of Dagon, and was undoubtedly a debased, quasi-pagan thing imported from the East a century before, at a time when the Innsmouth fisheries seemed to be going barren."

"THE SHADOW OVER INNSMOUTH", 1936

An ancient order who worship even older, mysterious creatures

"All in the band of the faithful – Order o' Dagon – an' the children shud never die, but go back to the Mother Hydra an' Father Dagon what we all come from onct – Iä! Iä! Cthulhu fhtagn! Ph'nglui mglw'nafh Cthulhu R'lyeh wgah-nagl fhtagn –"

ZADOK,
"THE SHADOW OVER INNSMOUTH", 1936
Recounting to the Narrator

"From that day on my life has been a nightmare of brooding and apprehension, nor do I know how much is hideous truth and how much madness."

"THE SHADOW OVER INNSMOUTH", 1936

A common element of mystery

"It is true that I have sent six bullets through the head of my best friend, and yet I hope to shew by this statement that I am not his murderer."

DANIEL UPTON,
"THE THING ON THE DOORSTEP", 1933
A stunning opening to any story

Ten Cthulhu deities

Abholos (Devourer in the Mist)

Ayi'ig (Serpent Goddess)

Coatlicue (Serpent Skirted One)

Yog-Sapha (Dweller of the Depths)

Zvilpogghua (Feaster from the Stars)

Shub-Niggurath (Black Goat of the Woods with a Thousand Young)

Yog-Sothoth (the All-in-One and One-in-All)

Nyarlathotep (the Crawling Chaos)

Nath-Horthath

Tamash

"She was one of the Innsmouth Waites, and dark legends have clustered for generations about crumbling, half-deserted Innsmouth and its people. There are tales of horrible bargains about the year 1850, and of a strange element – not quite human in the ancient families of the run-down fishing port."

DANIEL UPTON,
"THE THING ON THE DOORSTEP", 1933
Innsmouth makes another appearance

"Now she glares that way. And I know why! He found it in the *Necronomicon* – the formula."

EDWARD DERBY,
"THE THING ON THE DOORSTEP", 1933
To narrator Daniel Upton

"My brain! My brain! God, Dan – it's tugging – from beyond – knocking – clawing – that she- devil – even now – Ephraim – Kamog! Kamog! – The pit of the shoggoths – Iä! Shub- Niggurath! The Goat with a Thousand Young!"

EDWARD DERBY,
"THE THING ON THE DOORSTEP", 1933
Cthulhu's creatures make an appearance

"Can I be sure that I am safe? Those powers survive the life of the physical form."

DANIEL UPTON,
"THE THING ON THE DOORSTEP", 1933
Speaking of mysterious forces

"Assuming that I was sane and awake, my experience on that night was such as has befallen no man before."

NATHANIEL WINGATE PEASLEE,
"THE SHADOW OUT OF TIME", 1934

Those are big assumptions to make in any Lovecraft story...

"I went minutely through such things as the Comte d'Erlette's *Cultes des Goules*, Ludvig Prinn's *De Vermis Mysteriis*, the *Unaussprechlichen Kulten* of von Junzt, the surviving fragments of the puzzling *Book of Eibon*, and the dreaded *Necronomicon* of the mad Arab Abdul Alhazred."

NATHANIEL WINGATE PEASLEE,
"THE SHADOW OUT OF TIME", 1934
The narrator's (fictional) reading material

"There was, too, a feeling of profound and inexplicable horror concerning myself."

NATHANIEL WINGATE PEASLEE,
"THE SHADOW OUT OF TIME", 1934

The narrator has a fear of himself – or rather what may be inside

"I knew, too, that I had been snatched from my age while another used my body in that age, and that a few of the other strange forms housed similarly captured minds."

NATHANIEL WINGATE PEASLEE,
"THE SHADOW OUT OF TIME", 1934

Other bodies, other times

"Ph'nglui mglw'nafh Cthulhu R'lyeh wgah' nagl fhtagn."

[In his house at R'lyeh dead Cthulhu waits dreaming.]

"THE CALL OF CTHULHU", 1921

"NAMELESS"

Spawn of the Stars, Sofyan Syarief's artwork based on H. P. Lovecraft's story The Call of Cthulhu. Wikimedia Commons.

"Lights out – God help me."

ROBERT BLAKE,
"THE HAUNTER OF THE DARK", 1935

Blake's awful diary entry

"The full story, so far as deciphered, will shortly appear in an official bulletin of Miskatonic University."

WILLIAM DYER,
"AT THE MOUNTAINS OF MADNESS", 1931
An early reference to
Lovecraft's fictional university

"How it could have undergone its tremendously complex evolution on a new-born earth in time to leave prints in Archaean rocks was so far beyond conception as to make Lake whimsically recall the primal myths about Great Old Ones who filtered down from the stars and concocted earth-life as a joke or mistake."

WILLIAM DYER,
"AT THE MOUNTAINS OF MADNESS",1931

The ancient gods are no laughing matter

"The verdict, of course, was charlatanry. Somebody had played a joke on the superstitious hill-dwellers, or else some fanatic had striven to bolster up their fears for their own supposed good."

ROBERT BLAKE,
"THE HAUNTER OF THE DARK", 1935

Dismiss these mysterious tales
as a hoax at your peril

Cthulhu Mythos stories

As defined by Lin Carter in
Lovecraft: Behind the Cthulhu Mythos,
1972

"Dagon"

"Nyarlathotep"

"The Nameless City"

"The Hound"

"The Festival"

"The Call of Cthulhu"

"The Dunwich Horror"

"The Whisperer in Darkness"

"The Dreams in the Witch House"

"At the Mountains of Madness"

"The Shadow Over Innsmouth"

"The Shadow out of Time"

"The Haunter of the Dark"

"The Thing on the Doorstep"

"History of the Necronomicon" (essay)

"Fungi from Yuggoth" (poem)

CHAPTER

FOUR

"ANTIQUARIAN"

Although he is now famous for his "cosmic horror" writing, Lovecraft wrote for almost his entire life, on a variety of non-fiction subjects, as well as poetry, and tens of thousands of letters. Here we look at some of his lesser-known work, letters and more.

"How an Englishman fares within Dracula's stronghold of terrors, and how the dead fiend's plot for domination is at last defeated, are elements which unite to form a tale now justly assigned a permanent place in English letters."

H.P. LOVECRAFT,
"SUPERNATURAL HORROR IN LITERATURE",
1927
on Bram Stoker and *Dracula*

"The world is indeed comic, but the joke is on mankind."

H.P. LOVECRAFT
A typically barbed view of the state of man

The Colour Out of Space: Amazing Stories, September 1927.
Illustration by JM de Aragon. Wikimedia Commons.

"I can better understand the inert blindness and defiant ignorance of the reactionaries from having been one of them. I know how smugly ignorant I was – wrapped up in the arts, the natural (not social) sciences, the externals of history and antiquarianism, the abstract academic phases of philosophy, and so on..."

H.P. LOVECRAFT
In a letter to Catherine L. Moore, 1937

"The one test of the really weird is simply this – whether or not there be excited in the reader a profound sense of dread, and of contact with unknown spheres and powers..."

H.P. LOVECRAFT

Taking his writing incredibly seriously, as written in '*Supernatural Horror in Literature*', 1927

"Now all my tales are based on the fundamental premise that common human laws and interests and emotions have no validity or significance in the vast cosmos-at-large."

H.P. LOVECRAFT

An insight into what drove his writing, in a letter to Farnsworth Wright, 1927

"I certainly do not disagree with you concerning the essential solitude of the individual, for it seems to me the plainest of all truths that no highly organised and freely developed mind can possibly envisage an external world having much in common with the external world invisaged by any other mind."

H.P. LOVECRAFT
In a Letter to August Derleth, 1930

Examples of the writings of H.P. Lovecraft, journalist

Task for Amateur Journalists (1914)

For President–Leo Fritter (1915)

Amateurdom (1919)

Official Organ Fund (1921)

Lucubrations Lovecraftian (1921)

Rursus Adsumus (1923)

Lovecraft's Greeting (1923)

Verse Criticism (1933)

Mrs. Miniter–Estimates and Recollections (1938)

A Voice from the Grave (1941)

"My really favourite meal is the regular old New England turkey dinner, with highly seasoned dressing, cranberry sauce, onions, etc., and mince pie for dessert."

H.P. LOVECRAFT
On his preferred foodstuffs
Letter to Robert E. Howard, 1932

"Of other vegetables I like peas and onions, can tolerate cabbage and turnips, am neutral toward cauliflower, have no deep enmity toward carrots, prefer to dodge parsnips and asparagus, shun string beans and brussel sprouts and abominate spinach."

H.P. LOVECRAFT
Making his feelings on vegetables clear
Letter to J. Vernon Shea, 1931

"Memories and possibilities are ever more hideous than realities."

H.P. LOVECRAFT

Speaking his truth in fiction,
'Herbert West: Reanimator', 1922

"The dreams were wholly beyond the pale of sanity, and Gilman felt that they must be a result, jointly, of his studies in mathematics and in folklore."

H.P. LOVECRAFT

Showing multiple similarities with his characters, 'The Dreams in the Witch House', 1932

"Between dogs and cats my degree of choice is so great that it would never occur to me to compare the two. I have no active dislike for dogs ... but for the cat I have entertained a particular respect and affection ever since the earliest days of my infancy."

H.P. LOVECRAFT
He wrote an entire essay on canine and feline differences, 'Cats and Dogs', 1926

"To those who look beneath the surface, the present universal war drives home more than one anthropological truth in striking fashion; and of these verities none is more profound than that relating to the essential immutability of mankind and its instincts."

H.P. LOVECRAFT
Commenting on the Great War, 'At the Root', 1918

"How can anybody dislike *cheese*?"

H.P. LOVECRAFT
Lovecraft frequently discussed food, as here in a letter to J. Vernon Shea, 1931

"Hershey's sweet chocolate is one of my favourite nibbles."

H.P. LOVECRAFT
Commenting on his love of chocolate, in a letter to J. Vernon Shea, 1931

"But I more often take ice cream, of which my favourite flavours are vanilla and coffee ... my least relished common flavour is strawberry."

H.P. LOVECRAFT
And here too, on ice cream, in a letter to J. Vernon Shea, 1931

Lovecraft wrote frequently about science, including **"My Opinion as to the Lunar Canals"** (c. 1903), **"Does 'Vulcan' Exist"** (c. 1906) and **"The Falsity of Astrology"** (1914).

"Of all blunders, there is hardly one which might not be avoided through diligent study of simple textbooks on grammar and rhetoric, intelligent perusal of the best authors, and care and forethought in composition."

H.P. LOVECRAFT
He always had plenty to say about writing in general,
'Literary Composition', 1919

Lovecraft's travel writings include **"Homes and Shrines of Poe"** (1934) and **"Description of the Town of Quebeck in New-France, Lately added to His Britannick Majesty's Dominions"** (1931).

Lovecraft wrote many poems — long and short — from brief Christmas greetings to the terrifying epic "Fungi from Yuggoth".

"Wax not too frenzied in the leaping line
That neither sense nor measure can confine."

"THE POE-ET'S NIGHTMARE", 1918

"May good St. Nick, like as a bird of night,
Bring thee rich blessings in his annual flight"

"CHRISTMAS GREETINGS TO EUGENE B. KUNTZ ET AL."

"We are the valiant Knights of Peace
Who prattle for the Right..."

"PACIFIST WAR SONG—1917"

"Life! Ah, Life!
What may this fluorescent pageant mean?"

"LIFE'S MYSTERY"

"I shrieked – and knew what primal
star and year
Had sucked me back from man's
dream-transient sphere!"

"FUNGI FROM YUGGOTH", 1943

CHAPTER FIVE

"INFLUENCE"

Despite a literary career that was limited in scope and success, H.P. Lovecraft became a household name in horror. But his influence was felt much farther afield, in music, games, and of course literature.

"Arkham Asylum was named for a somewhat similar facility known as 'Arkham Sanitarium' mentioned in the horror fiction of Howard Phillips Lovecraft."

DAVID WELLS
Batman Unauthorized: Vigilantes,
Jokers, and Heroes in Gotham City, edited by Dennis O'Neil,
Smart Pop, 2008

"Behind the Wall of Sleep is a reference to the H.P. Lovecraft short story 'Beyond the Wall of Sleep'."

DAVID WELLS
Black Sabbath CD booklet, Sanctuary Records, 2009

H.P. Lovecraft wrote "In Memoriam: Robert Ervin Howard" following the death (by suicide) of his great friend Robert E. Howard, creator of "Conan the Barbarian".

"When you read more widely about the guy you see he loved his friends, he loved Providence, he loved the landscape around him, he was not a cold man."

ALAN MOORE

All About Alienation: Alan Moore on Lovecraft and Providence by Nick Talbot, 2014

Ten Lovecraft-inspired writers

Neil Gaiman – *I Cthulhu*

Peter Straub – *A Dark Matter*

Ramsey Campbell (ed.) – *New Tales of the Cthulhu Mythos*

Marc Laidlaw – *The 37th Mandala*

Stephen King – *From a Buick 8*

William Meikle – *The Amulet*

Briane Keen and Nick Mamatas – *The Damned Highway*

Laird Barron – *The Croning*

Matt Ruff – *Lovecraft Country*

Jacqueline Baker – *The Broken Hours*

"In the Mouth of Madness is, therefore, not just a love letter to the late H.P. Lovecraft and his tales of cosmic terror, but also a thorough and thoroughly visceral examination of the influence fictional worlds can have on the internal world, or dare I say reality, of the consumer."

KORALJKA SUTON
Commenting on John Carpenter's *In the Mouth of Madness*, Cinephilia and Beyond

"Overall, it was an homage to the work of H.P. Lovecraft, crossed with the detective genre and a few western elements."

JOHN CARPENTER
On *In the Mouth of Madness*

"We thought we had a very good, safe package. It was $150 [million], Tom Cruise and James Cameron producing, ILM doing the effects, here's the art, this is the concept, because I really think big-scale horror would be great."

GUILLERMO DEL TORO

On his as yet unrealized project *At the Mountains of Madness*, 2017

Popular Lovecraft stories

"The Call of Cthulhu"

"The Shadow Over Innsmouth"

"The Whisperer in Darkness"

"At the Mountains of Madness"

"The Case of Charles Dexter Ward"

"The Dunwich Horror"

"Dagon"

"Herbert West – Reanimator"

"The Color Out of Space"

"The Rats in the Walls"

"INFLUENCE"

The Colour Out of Space: Amazing Stories, 1927.
Illustration by JM de Aragon. Wikimedia Commons.

Ten Lovecraft-inspired video games

Stygian: Reign of the Old Ones

Eldritch

The Secret World

Gray Dawn

The Sinking City

Call of Cthulhu

Darkwood

Curse of the Old Gods

Necronomicon: The Dawning of Darkness

Eternal Darkness: Sanity's Requiem

"I've reread Lovecraft over the decades and have found even more to admire – the careful complex structures, the modulation of the prose (quite the reverse of the parodic version of his style even some of his admirers promulgate.)"

RAMSEY CAMPBELL
2020

"Tellingly he said that his entities should not be seen as evil. He said things like 'good' 'evil' 'love' 'hate' – these are all human concepts that mean nothing to the vast infinities."

ALAN MOORE
All About Alienation: Alan Moore on Lovecraft and Providence by Nick Talbot, 2014

Necronomicon Ex-Mortis (*The Book of the Dead*) from the *Evil Dead* movies was first mentioned (as the *Necronomicon*) by H.P. Lovecraft in "The Hound", 1924.

"Lovecraft's horrors, as Fritz Leiber rightly asserted, actually embodies what Rudolf Otto described as the very essence of religion: the non-rational, non-moral experience of the Numinous, a dipolar experience of the Mysterium Tremendum and the Mysterium Fascinans."

ROBERT M. PRICE

"He's a great American writer. His work has proved very durable. I think people will be reading him for as long as people read."

PETER STRAUB
2005

The Nameless City. Illustration by Angela Sprecher's . Wikimedia Commons.

Ten Lovecraft-inspired movies

Dagon (2001)
The Call of Cthulhu (2005)
The Thing (1982)
From Beyond (1986)
Re-Animator (1985)
Hellraiser (1987)
In the Mouth of Madness (1994)
The Resurrected (1991)
City of the Living Dead (1980)
The Dunwich Horror (1970)

Lovecraft Country is an HBO television series about a young black man travelling across a segregated United States in the 1950s.

It includes many places from H.P. Lovecraft's life and writings.

"The point it cleverly makes is that supernatural entities are nothing compared with the ancient wickedness of racial oppression in America. Monsters can be outfought and out-thought. Racism, by contrast, is impossible to banish. Lovecraft would have hated it, which merely adds to the appeal."

ED POWER

Writing on racism in Lovecraft Country, *The Irish Times*, 2020

Fictional books from Lovecraft stories

Liber Ivonis

Cultes des Goules by Comte d'Erlette

Unaussprechlichen Kulten by von Junzt

De Vermis Mysteriis by Ludvig Prinn

The Pnakotic Manuscripts

The Book of Dzyan

"a crumbling volume in wholly unidentifiable characters yet with certain symbols and diagrams shudderingly recognisable to the occult student"

"Lovecraft was absolutely one of the most accomplished 'world builders' in imaginative fiction."

S.T. JOSHI
2017

"**H.P.** Lovecraft was racist, antisemitic, misogynist, and deeply fucked up."

NEIL GAIMAN
Twitter, 2020

H.P. Lovecraft's most popular words

10. **Loath** (-ing/-some) - 71
9. **Accursed** - 76
8. **Blasphem** (-y/-ous) - 92
7. **Abnormal** - 94
6. **Madness** - 115
5. **Singular** (-ly) - 115
4. **Antiqu** (-e/-arian) - 128
3. **Nameless** - 157
2. **Faint** (-ed/-ing) - 189
1. **Hideous** - 260

"The Shadow Over Innsmouth" was the only story by H.P. Lovecraft that was published as a book during his lifetime.

"I feel like too many people are obsessed with Lovecraft's monsters, tentacles and polyps and shuggoths ... I think they're missing the point. At least, I can say they're missing the part that has played the greatest influence on me ... the importance of atmosphere, the found manuscript as a narrative device, and his appreciation of what paleontologists and geologists call deep time."

CAITLÍN R. KIERNAN
2012

"I never ask a man what his business is, for it never interests me. What I ask him about are his thoughts and dreams."

H.P. LOVECRAFT